Atul's Christmas Hamster

Richard Brown

Illustrated by Paul Howard

CAMBRIDGE
UNIVERSITY PRESS

One day, when I was six, a friend showed me his hamster.

All the way home that day, I thought,
"I want a hamster, too."

A few days later, Mum said, "What do you want for Christmas, Atul?"

"I want a hamster," I said.

"Oh dear," said Mum.

"Are you sure?" said Dad. "You'll have to feed it and keep it clean."

"Please?" I asked.

"We'll think about it," they said.

I didn't know if they were going to buy me
a hamster or not. So every day I kept watch,
to see if they brought one home.

Soon, Christmas was only two days away.
There was still no sign of any hamster.

"Please?" I asked again.

"We're still thinking about it," said Dad.

Later that day, I saw Dad give a big box
to our neighbour.

"What's that box?" I asked him when
he came in.

But Dad wouldn't tell me.

On Christmas Eve, we put up the
decorations.

Then Mum got her bike out to go shopping.

"Are you going to buy me a hamster?"
I asked.

"We're still thinking about it," said Mum.

When Mum came back, Dad said,
"Wait in here, Atul."

I saw them lift a small box from
Mum's bike.

"What's that box for?" I asked, when they came in.

"What box?" they said. It had gone.
They must have hidden it.

On Christmas morning, I ran into Mum
and Dad's bedroom.

"Look under the Christmas tree," said Mum.
"You'll find a big present there for you."

"Open it very carefully," said Dad.

On the parcel was a card which said,
"To Atul, with love from Mum, Dad and
Sangeeta."

I tore off the paper.

Wow! It was a cage – a cage for a hamster.
At last!

But where was the hamster?

"I expect he's still asleep under that heap of paper," said Mum.

"Wait for half an hour or so," said Dad. "He'll soon wake up."

So I waited half an hour by the cage.

"Can't we wake him up?" I asked, again
and again.

Mum lifted the lid and felt about in the
paper. "I can't feel him in there," she said.

"He's very small," said Dad. "Wait for a
bit longer."

So I waited. I waited a whole hour.

Mum looked again. "Oh no!" she cried.
"The hamster's not in there. He must have
got out in the night."

We spent hours looking for him. We even looked in the garden.

"He must have run away," said Mum.

"If he has, we'll get you another one," said Dad.

"I want *this* one," I said, and I kept looking for him for most of that Christmas Day.

That night, I felt really sad.

On Boxing Day, Mum was cooking in
the kitchen. She said, "Fetch some carrots,
please, Atul."

I opened the cupboard door. And there,
on a pile of chewed carrots, was . . .

. . . my hamster! There he was, curled up, fast asleep and full of carrot.